Ariel

The Shimmering
Star Necklace

visit us at www.abdopublishing.com

Reinforced library bound edition published in 2014 by Spotlight, a division of the ABDO Group, PO Box 398166, Minneapolis, MN 55439. Spotlight produces high-quality reinforced library bound editions for schools and libraries. Published by agreement with Disney Press.

Printed in the United States of America, North Mankato, Minnesota.
102013
012014

 This book contains at least 10% recycled materials.

Library of Congress Cataloging-in-Publication Data
This title was previously cataloged with the following information:
Herman, Gail.
  Ariel the shimmering star necklace by Gail Herman ; illustrated by Emilio Urbano, Manuela Razzi, and the Disney Storybook Artists.
  p. cm. -- (Disney Princess)
  Summary: Ariel's sisters have given her a beautiful present --a shimmering star-shell necklace. Ariel can't wait to wear it to the royal concert. But when the concert's lead singer, a young girl named Laurel, suddenly disappears, it's up to Ariel and her friends to find her.
  1. Disney characters--Juvenile fiction. 2. Princesses--Juvenile fiction. I. Title. II Series.
PZ7.H Ar 2012
[Fic]--dc23   2011934216

ISBN 978-1-61479-211-6 (Reinforced Library Bound Edition)

All Spotlight books are reinforced library binding and manufactured in the United States of America.

Ariel

The Shimmering Star Necklace

By Gail Herman
Illustrated by Emilio Urbano,
Manuela Razzi, and the Disney Storybook Artists

New York

Chapter One

$\mathcal{A}$riel walked along a cobblestoned path. The road wound around the village square, where shop owners were selling colorful jewelry, scarves, and trinkets.

"Lovely morning, isn't it, Princess?" the town baker called as Ariel passed by.

"Yes, it is!" Ariel smiled.

It was a Saturday, and the village was bustling with activity. Ariel just loved

strolling through the town square in the warm sunshine.

She stopped at a corner to read a sign.

The Village School Presents:
A special concert for
our Royal Family~
Join us next Saturday!

Just one week until the concert! Ariel quickened her step. She was on her way to a special appointment, and she didn't want to be late.

A few blocks from the village center, Ariel walked up to a small white cottage. Daisies dotted the lawn and roses filled the flower boxes.

Ariel knocked on the door.

A young girl answered. "Princess Ariel! You're here!" she exclaimed. "I can't believe you're really going to help me practice for the concert. I'm Laurel, your music student. And I'm going to work really hard. I promise."

Ariel laughed. Laurel was certainly very excited!

The young girl's father, Mr. Hansen, came to the door. "Now that Princess Ariel is here," he said gently to his daughter, "why don't you go gather your music?"

Ariel smiled as Laurel ran back into the house. "It's nice to meet you both," she said to Mr. Hansen. "I'm so glad Laurel's teacher asked me to help her rehearse."

The town school was hosting a royal concert the next Saturday, and Laurel had been chosen to sing a solo. Miss Summers, Laurel's teacher, knew Ariel was a wonderful singer. So she had asked Ariel if she would like to help the young girl practice a song for the concert.

"I'd love to!" Ariel had answered.

Laurel returned with an armful of music.

"Are you ready to begin?" Ariel asked.

"Oh, yes!" Laurel exclaimed.

In the parlor, Ariel sat down at the piano in the center of the room. She opened one of the music books and pointed to a page. "This is Prince Eric's favorite song," she said.

"'The Song of the Sea,'" Laurel read the title aloud. "It's my favorite, too!"

"Shall we try practicing it?" Ariel asked.

Together, they sang through the whole piece while Ariel played the piano. "You have a beautiful voice," Ariel told Laurel.

The young girl grinned happily. Then she leaned closer. "You know what, Princess Ariel? I have a feeling my new friend would like this song a lot, too."

"Oh, really?" Ariel asked. "What's your friend's name?"

Laurel opened her mouth to answer. Then she hesitated. She tucked her short brown hair behind her ears. "Um, I don't think

you'd know her. I only met her the other day. But I really like her!"

"That's wonderful," Ariel said. "It's always important to make new friends."

Laurel glanced at the clock. "I'm meeting

her right after our lesson," she said. "I don't know what we'll do, exactly. But I know it will be fun!"

Again, Laurel checked the time. "Do you think we'll be practicing much longer, Princess Ariel?"

Ariel laughed. "We've just started, but we'll go as quickly as we can. I think 'The Song of the Sea' is the perfect choice for the concert. Let's sing it together one more time."

$\mathcal{A}$riel worked with Laurel every day that week. Finally, the morning of the concert arrived. Ariel had one last lesson with the young girl. But that wasn't going to be until after lunch. So she decided to visit with her sisters out by the ocean for a while.

Ariel's sisters were all mermaids. Not long ago, Ariel had been a mermaid, too. But then she had fallen in love with Prince

Eric, who was a human. Ariel's father, King Triton, had seen how much Ariel and Eric loved one another. He had transformed Ariel into a human so that she and Eric could be together. Ariel loved her life as a human, but she sometimes missed being under the sea with her sisters.

Excited, she walked to the shore. When she reached the edge of the water, she called out, "Attina! Alana! Adella! Aquata! Arista! Andrina! Hello! I'm here!"

A moment later, the sound of voices echoed over the waves.

"Ariel! Hello! It's us!"

Her six sisters waved from out in the water. Ariel gathered her skirts and walked along a row of rocks jutting far out into the sea. Everyone swam up to meet her.

"Look what we brought you!" Aquata announced. "An under-the-sea snack!" She held up a picnic basket made from reeds. Inside were seashell plates piled high with sugared seaweed.

"How wonderful!" Ariel exclaimed. "I love sugared seaweed!"

"Aren't you glad I thought of having a picnic?" Aquata asked proudly.

"What do you mean *you* thought of it?" snapped Alana. "I thought of it!"

"No, you didn't," Aquata retorted.

"Yes, I did!"

"It's all right!" Ariel interrupted. "No matter who thought of it, I'm sure it will be delicious."

As the sisters ate, they told Ariel all the ocean news. "So the turtles held a surprise birthday party for Myrtle, who just turned one hundred and sixty-three! And she loved the shell polish we gave her!" Andrina finished the update.

Afterward, Ariel dipped her feet in the water. She watched her sisters splash and swim. Alana and Aquata dove deep into the waves.

"Look at this!" The two sisters suddenly popped up together. Each held the edge of a shell. It had five points and was very delicate. In the sunlight, it almost looked like it was glowing.

"That's a star shell!" breathed Adella. "I can't believe you found one. They're so rare!"

"They're supposed to grant wishes." Andrina said excitedly. "I remember singing the rhyme when we were little:

"One star, one shell, one wish is all.

For more wishes, more stars must fall."

"Then someone else would sing the next line," added Adella.

"Two stars, two shells, two wishes all.

For more wishes, more stars must fall."

"And on and on," Arista continued. "But how would it end?"

For a moment the sisters were silent. "I think there was another part to the rhyme," Ariel said slowly. "A line we'd all recite together. But I can't remember it!" She paused. "I do remember Father telling us the legend of the magic star shell when we were little."

"Can you tell us now?" asked Attina.

Ariel nodded. Her sisters settled around her.

"A very long time ago," Ariel began, "a magical light filled the skies above Atlantica. Shooting stars fell one by one into the water. Some dropped to the ocean floor. Others got tangled in reeds and sea grass. But some

stars struck seashells. And they burned with a shimmering light. They were transformed into star shells.

"Legend has it," Ariel continued, "that the first wish made on a star shell comes true."

"Maybe we found a new star shell!" Andrina said excitedly.

"We could make a wish!" cried Adella.

Ariel smiled. "It's just a story, remember? Then again . . ." She gazed at the star shell thoughtfully. "Shall we find out if the legend is really true?"

"Yes!" the sisters cried together.

"I found it," Aquata said. "I'll make the wish."

"No!" Alana pounded her tail against the water. "I found it. I should make the wish."

"Me."

"No, me!"

Aquata's and Alana's voices grew louder and louder.

Andrina took hold of the star shell. "I wish you would both stop talking!" she shouted.

Everyone gasped. Would Andrina's wish come true?

Chapter Three

$\mathcal{A}$ndrina clapped her hand over her mouth. Alana and Aquata looked horrified.

"Relax," Ariel said. "I'm sure it's just a legend. Go ahead and say something."

"It's all your fault, Alana," exclaimed Aquata.

"No, it's your fault!" cried Alana.

Andrina laughed, relieved. "Well, I guess the magic star shell is just a legend after all. It didn't grant my wish."

"Or else it's already been used," Ariel added. "Either way, we're lucky!"

"Yes, we're lucky, and we're late!" Arista said. "Father is waiting for us. We're having cousins Bettina and Benita over for a visit."

"That sounds like fun," Ariel said. Her expression grew slightly sad. "I'm sorry I can't go, too. I miss spending time with all of you under the water."

Aquata and Alana looked at one another.

"Here, Ariel." Alana handed her the shell. "You should keep it. And look, it even has a hole at the top. You could make it into a necklace."

"Thank you!" Ariel said. "Now I'll carry a piece of the sea wherever I go!"

A short while later, Ariel was on her way to Laurel's house. The star shell shone brightly around her neck. She had found a delicate ribbon to loop through the hole at the top to make a necklace. She couldn't wait to wear it to the concert that night.

She was also looking forward to working with Laurel. It was their last rehearsal!

Soon Ariel came to the cottage. But the door was already open, swaying slightly in the breeze. That's odd, Ariel thought.

"Princess Ariel! Princess Ariel!" a voice called from behind her.

Ariel turned to see Laurel's father. He was hurrying up the walkway. "Is Laurel with you?" he asked. He sounded upset.

Ariel shook her head. "No. Is something wrong?"

Mr. Hansen didn't answer. Instead he ran inside the house. "Laurel?" he called. "Are you home now?"

Ariel quickly followed him inside. "What's happened?"

Mr. Hansen's face looked pale. "Laurel went out this morning to play with a friend," he explained. "She said she would be home in time for lunch. But she never came back!"

"Did you check with her friend?" Ariel asked.

Laurel's father nodded. "I did—at least, I tried. I thought she was seeing Joanna, her friend from class. I thought she'd been going to her house after school all week.

"But just now I talked to Joanna's mother. She told me Laurel wasn't there. And worse, it hasn't been their house Laurel's been going to each afternoon, either."

Mr. Hansen sighed. "It's not at all like Laurel to just run off. She knew about your lesson, and she wanted to rehearse before the concert tonight. Something must be wrong."

"Don't worry," Ariel said. "I'm sure we'll find her. Are there any other friends she would be playing with? Or does she have any new . . ."

Suddenly, Ariel stopped. "I just remembered something!" she exclaimed. "When I first met Laurel, she told me about a new friend she had just started seeing. Do you know who it could be?"

"A *new* friend?" Laurel's father shook his head. "Laurel didn't say anything to me. Does she live in the village?"

"I have no idea." Ariel shrugged. "Laurel didn't even tell me her name. But there has to be a way to figure this out. Maybe we can find a clue. Can we look in Laurel's room?"

"Of course," Mr. Hansen agreed.

They both hurried to Laurel's bedroom. Ariel walked over to a small wooden desk against the wall. Drawings covered every inch. There were pictures of castles and farms and animals.

"Those are Laurel's sketches from school," Mr. Hansen said. "Laurel loves drawing."

Ariel opened one of the desk drawers. "What's this?" she asked, pulling out a pretty book with a pink cover.

"That's Laurel's diary," Mr. Hansen said. "She writes in it every night."

"Maybe she wrote about her new friend!" Ariel said hopefully. "Then we can find out who she is!"

Chapter Four

"I feel bad about reading this without Laurel knowing," Mr. Hansen said. "But it could be important." They quickly flipped to the last few entries and read:

Dear Diary,

Something great happened today! I can't tell anyone about it. Not even Daddy. I met a new friend! I was walking home from school, and I started chasing a butterfly. It flew all the way to the end of Wavestone Path. I've never been down that far before. That's where I met my new friend! At first, I thought it was a girl from my class. But then I realized that I didn't know her. "My name is Calista," she told me. "Do you want to play with me?"

Calista said she had always wanted a friend like me, but that I shouldn't tell anyone we had met. We pretended to go on all sorts of adventures!

Feeling excited, Ariel read the next entry.

Dear Diary,

I'm sorry I didn't write more this week. I

have been so busy playing with Calista every day after school.

But today was the best day of all. Calista gave me a beautiful necklace! I'd like to show it to my friends at school. And especially Princess Ariel. But Calista said not to tell anyone about our secret friendship. She's not sure we're supposed to be playing together.

I like having a secret friend. It's more exciting that way. I think I'll get her a present, too. Tomorrow, I'll go to the pastry shop after school and buy her a treat. Something I just know she will like. She'll be so surprised!

That was where the diary ended. "Well," Ariel said. She gave Mr. Hansen an encouraging smile. "That gives us some clues. The friend Laurel's been playing with is named Calista. And they met at the end of Wavestone Path."

"Wavestone Path?" Mr. Hansen repeated. "Is that where Calista lives? We hardly ever go over there."

"I know where it is," Ariel said. She shook her head. "There aren't any houses there. But it's worth going to take a look. If they've been playing there all week, there might be some more clues."

"And I'll check the village again," said Mr. Hansen. "I'll ask people if they know Calista."

"We'll find Laurel," Ariel promised. "And before you know it, she'll be home, getting ready for the concert."

But first, Ariel said to herself, looking at the diary, we need to find Calista. She holds the key to everything!

Chapter Five

A short while later, Ariel had reached the end of Wavestone Path. It was just as she remembered it—a long row of pebbles leading out to the ocean. Not a house or person in sight. Ariel sighed. Well, Calista certainly can't live here, she said to herself. Just then, she heard a loud squawking noise. She jumped and looked up.

"Ariel?" a voice called.

"Scuttle? Is that you?" she asked.

"Of course it's me," the seagull said. He quickly flew up and settled on a rock. "Who else would be flying around calling your name?"

Ariel laughed. She and Scuttle were good friends. When she was a mermaid, he used to tell her all about the human world. And Ariel was always glad to see him. Maybe he could help her right now.

"I like your neck brace," Scuttle said, admiring Ariel's shimmering star-shell necklace. "Will you be wearing it to a formal event?"

"Well, I am going to the school concert tonight," Ariel said. "Tell me, Scuttle, have you seen two little girls playing here? Maybe this morning?"

"Two girls?" Scuttle scratched his head. "I don't think so. Unless *you* count. In which case, I've seen one girl here today. But not two."

"No, not me. I'm looking for a missing girl named Laurel," Ariel told Scuttle. "She was supposed to sing in the school concert tonight, but now we can't find her. Her diary said something about meeting a friend here."

"Aha!" exclaimed Scuttle. He nodded his head, trying to look wise. "I know all about diaries! Those flowers are so pretty. And so useful. When you pick the petals, they'll tell you if he loves you. Or if he loves you not."

Ariel shook her head and giggled. "That's a daisy, Scuttle. A diary is a book."

"Well, of course it is!" Scuttle agreed. "It's

a special book filled with definitions."

Ariel sighed. "That's a dictionary, Scuttle. A diary is a book that you write in, telling it about your feelings and what you do all day." She held out Laurel's diary to show him.

"So what did this Laurel do all day?" Scuttle asked, looking closely at the journal.

"Well, she visited this spot and she met

a friend," Ariel said. "But I haven't seen a single person here. This place is deserted!"

"Desserted! How can you say that?" Scuttle asked. "Do you see any desserts here? Any clam-juice cupcakes? Sea-jelly doughnuts? No!"

Scuttle looked very satisfied with himself. This time, he knew he was right. "For a place to be desserted, you'd have to have desserts!"

"Scuttle!" Ariel cried. "You just gave me an idea!" She kissed him on the beak. "Laurel bought dessert for Calista! Maybe the baker knows something. I'll go to the pastry shop right now!"

"The pastry shop? Ho, ho," Scuttle chuckled as Ariel rushed away toward the village. "Paste is a very strange dessert. It might be a little tough to eat. Sticking to your mouth and all. But I guess there's no accounting for taste, is there?"

<hr />

Ariel ran all the way to the village center. Outside the pastry shop, she caught her breath. Then she pushed open the door. Delicious smells filled the air. Bread baking. A whiff of chocolate. Vanilla cupcakes. Ariel's stomach rumbled.

"Hello, Princess Ariel!" cried Hans the baker. "What a nice surprise. Would you like a sweet blueberry tart, fresh from the oven? Perhaps a muffin for Prince Eric? Or a dog biscuit for Max?"

"Well, maybe a honey bun," Ariel said. She couldn't resist! She put some coins on the counter. When Hans brought her the bun, she took a few nibbles. The honey was deliciously sweet and sticky.

"Thank you, Hans." She smiled. "I'm here to ask you a question as well." She quickly explained how Laurel had gone missing.

Hans rubbed his hands together, thinking. Flour flew from his fingertips. "Yes, I do remember Laurel," he finally said. "She came in the other day. She asked for seaweed puffs!" The baker shook his head. "Can you imagine?"

"Seaweed puffs?" Ariel asked, surprised. "Why would Laurel want those?"

Hans shrugged as he rang up another

customer. "I wanted to help the little girl. You know, she talks and talks, but she's very sweet. Anyway, I gave her a cream pastry with a piece of seaweed around it. Hopefully, she enjoyed it." A worried look crossed his face. "You said you can't find her?"

Ariel shook her head. "No, but I'm sure we'll figure out where she is. Thank you for your help, and the honey bun."

Ariel was just about to leave when a mother and daughter came up to the counter. The daughter looked about Laurel's age.

"Hello, ladies," the baker said. The little girl smiled and handed him a card.

Hans opened it. "Why, it's a thank-you note!" he exclaimed. He showed it to Ariel.

The card was drawn in colored pencils. It said:

Thank you for baking my
yummy birthday cake!
Your friend,
Maggie

"You are very welcome." Hans smiled.

"Maggie wrote the note for a school assignment yesterday," Maggie's mother explained. "Each student had to make a thank-you card for a friend. When I told Maggie we were coming to the bakery, she was so excited. She wanted to give her card to you right away! So we stopped by the school to pick it up. Lucky for us, Miss Summers was there to let us in."

Ariel gasped. Miss Summers was Laurel's schoolteacher! She knelt to speak to Maggie. "Do you know a girl named Calista?" she asked.

Maggie shook her head.

"Do you know Laurel?"

"Yes," the little girl said. "She's in my class."

"Have you seen her today?" Ariel asked.

"No," Maggie said. "But she was in school on Friday."

Maybe Miss Summers knows who Calista is, Ariel thought. She could be in another class. Suddenly, Ariel remembered something Laurel had written in her diary. She opened the book and read a line from the last entry again.

Calista gave me a gift. A beautiful necklace.

Maybe Laurel wrote a thank-you note to her new friend! Ariel thought to herself excitedly. "Are the other thank-you notes still at the school?" she asked Maggie's mother.

The woman nodded. "I imagine they would be. Maggie's was there."

"Perfect!" Ariel cried. She hugged Maggie. "I should write *you* a thank-you note for helping me!" she said.

Maggie blushed.

"Good-bye!" Ariel said, racing away.

"Wait! Your honey bun!" Hans called after her. But Ariel was already out the door.

Chapter Six

$\mathcal{A}$riel rushed to the village school. "Oh, I hope Miss Summers is still there!" she said. "I need to find those thank-you cards!"

At the school gate, she stepped up to the heavy double doors and pulled on the handles. They were locked!

Now what? Ariel thought. She sat on the front step, her chin cupped in her hands.

"Excuse me, Princess Ariel?"

Ariel turned toward the voice.

Laurel's teacher, Miss Summers, was standing at the doors. "I was in the cellar, making sure we had enough chairs for the concert tonight. But I thought I heard someone outside."

"Oh, Miss Summers. I'm so glad you're here!" Ariel exclaimed.

The woman smiled. "Are you meeting Laurel here for her lesson?"

"Actually, I'm looking for her," Ariel said as she followed the teacher inside. "We can't find her anywhere."

"Laurel is missing?" Miss Summers' eyes opened wide. "How terrible! Is there anything I can do?"

"Yes!" Ariel replied. "We think Laurel

might be with a friend named Calista. Do you know her?"

"Calista?" Miss Summers shook her head. "The name doesn't sound familiar at all."

Ariel's heart sank. But there was still the thank-you card assignment. "Maggie's mother mentioned that your students wrote thank-you notes the other day. I was hoping Laurel might have written one to Calista?"

"Well, let's see," Miss Summers said, quickly walking down the hall and into a classroom with Ariel. She opened a box filled with notes on her desk. One by one, she looked them over before pulling out a pretty yellow card.

"Here's Laurel's," she said. Eagerly, Ariel began to read:

Laurel had drawn a picture of herself on the left side of the card. She was riding a musical note that looked like a horse. Ariel was holding the reins, leading. A rainbow of smaller musical notes arched around them.

Ariel sighed. It was so sweet of Laurel to thank her. And the drawing was lovely. But the note wasn't for Calista. Ariel had been so sure the card would hold a clue.

She touched the shimmering star shell hanging from her neck. If only she could wish for Laurel to come home.

Miss Summers read the card over Ariel's shoulder. "Oh!" she said, disappointed. "The card is for you. I'm sorry."

The teacher looked closely at the picture. "Laurel really is my star student. Look at this drawing! She has such an imagination."

"She certainly does," Ariel said.

"I ask my students to draw a picture each day," Miss Summers continued. "Just yesterday, I had the class draw pictures called 'My Best Friend.' Laurel couldn't wait to get started."

My Best Friend? Ariel exclaimed. She and Miss Summers looked at one another.

"Maybe she drew a picture of Calista!" they said at the same time.

"I haven't had time to look at them," Miss Summers said, quickly pulling out another box. She flipped through the drawings. "Oh, dear," she said. "Laurel's seems to be missing."

"Oh!" Ariel sighed. If only she had that picture. It had to be of Calista!

And all at once, Ariel remembered Laurel's room. Drawings had covered her desk. Pictures of castles and farms . . . and maybe friends!

"I just had an idea that I think will help us find that picture," Ariel said excitedly. "Thank you so much for your help, Miss Summers. I'm sure I'll see you tonight at the concert—with Laurel!"

In no time at all, Ariel was back at Laurel's house. Mr. Hansen opened the door.

"I couldn't find out anything in the village," he said. "Do you have news?"

"Yes!" Ariel said breathlessly. "The clues from Laurel's diary led me all around town. She drew a picture . . . it might be of Calista . . . and it might be here! In your house!"

"Let's go!" Mr. Hansen cried.

They went straight to Laurel's room. Ariel quickly examined each drawing on the desk. She found a picture of Mr. Hansen with the title "My Family." A picture of her cottage, labeled "My Home." And another of the town center, called "My Village." But not one drawing of a friend.

"Maybe Laurel hid the picture," she said to Mr. Hansen. "Remember, she was trying to keep Calista a secret."

They searched under the bed, inside the desk, and beneath the rug. Nothing. Ariel sat back on the floor. "Now what?" she asked.

"We can't give up!" Laurel's father said anxiously.

"Of course not," Ariel agreed. "There's

got to be something we're missing. One final clue."

Idly, she picked up a music book. It seemed so long ago that she and Laurel had practiced "The Song of the Sea."

Suddenly, a folded piece of paper fell out from between the pages.

Laurel's father picked it up. "This is it!" he gasped. "It's—oh, my . . ."

"What? What is it?" Ariel cried. Not saying a word, Mr. Hansen held out the paper.

It was the "My Best Friend" picture. Two girls were in the drawing. One was Laurel, with short brown hair and a wide smile. And the other girl had wavy blond hair. It had to be Calista.

And she was a mermaid.

Chapter Seven

"Could this be true?" Laurel's father asked. "Could her new friend be a mermaid?"

Ariel thought for a moment. "It does all make sense," she said slowly. "Look at the clues. Laurel met Calista at the end of Wavestone Path. But Wavestone Path ends at the ocean. That could mean Calista lives in the water!"

"I suppose that's possible." Laurel's father nodded.

"Then there's the bakery," Ariel said. "Laurel wanted to buy Calista seaweed puffs. She must have thought that they would be the perfect treat for a mermaid."

Mr. Hansen frowned. "But why would Calista tell my daughter to keep her a secret? Forgive me, Princess, but after you married Prince Eric, I thought mermaids were no longer hidden from humans."

Ariel laughed. "You're right. *I'm* certainly not a secret. But merpeople don't come to the surface very often. Calista might have thought she'd get in trouble for playing with Laurel."

Mr. Hansen nodded thoughtfully. Then he pointed back to the picture. "What is that around Laurel's neck?"

Ariel looked back at the picture and gasped. Laurel was wearing a very familiar-looking necklace. "It's a star shell!" Ariel exclaimed. She touched the matching necklace she was wearing. "They're very rare. My sisters just gave me this one as a present this morning. Calista must have found another and given it to Laurel."

"I don't believe it, but it must be true," Laurel's father said. "Calista is a mermaid!" He looked at Ariel. "But if Calista is a mermaid, then where is my daughter?"

"There's only one way to find out," Ariel said. "Come on!"

Together, they rushed out of the house and ran all the way to the end of Wavestone Path, straight to the ocean.

"Sebastian! Flounder!" Ariel called out over the water once they had reached the shore. "Can either of you hear me? Are you nearby?"

Both Ariel and Mr. Hansen turned as they heard splashing. It was Sebastian, scrambling up on a rock. Just behind him, Flounder leaped from the waves.

"We're here, Ariel!" Sebastian called. He huffed and puffed. "Now what's so

important? I was just gathering some fresh reed batons." He made a slight bow. "You do know I've written some new pieces featuring the harp and the castanets? And your father thinks they're my finest work." Sebastian's chest swelled with pride. "Is that why you're calling? To join the ensemble?"

"That can't be it! You want to go exploring. Right, Ariel?" Flounder bounced in the water. "You want to go to a shipwreck? Or a cave? Tell us, Ariel. Tell us!"

"No, it's nothing like that," Ariel said. "I need to go under the sea right away. Can you find Daddy for me?"

"Right away!" Sebastian said, growing serious. He turned to Flounder. "You swim around Atlantica. I'll check the palace!"

Flounder nodded. "We'll find him! You can count on us, Ariel!"

Flounder dove into a wave. He moved quickly, swimming for all he was worth . . . in the wrong direction.

"You're heading toward shore, Flounder!" Sebastian cried. He sighed deeply. "Oh, what I have to put up with! Now follow me!"

"Thank you!" Ariel called as her friends disappeared into the water.

Ariel and Mr. Hansen didn't have to wait long. King Triton surfaced just minutes later. Flounder and Sebastian were by his side.

"Is something wrong, Ariel?" he asked at once.

"I'm fine, Daddy," she told him. She gestured to Laurel's father. "But Mr. Hansen's daughter, Laurel, is missing." She explained about Laurel and Calista, and showed her father the picture.

"We think Calista might know where Laurel is. Can you change me into a mermaid?" she asked.

"Yes, of course," King Triton replied. He turned to Mr. Hansen. "You must be very worried."

"I am, sir, er, Your Highness," Mr. Hansen stammered. "Thank you very much for offering to help."

Ariel gave Mr. Hansen a reassuring smile. "Just wait here, and we'll be back as soon as we've found Calista. I promise we won't be long."

Mr. Hansen stepped back as King Triton

raised his trident high in the air.

At the same time, Ariel dove into the water. Her legs disappeared, transforming into a tail. Ariel flipped her fin. It always felt good to swim!

"Where should we start?" King Triton asked as they swam into the depths.

"We have to find out where Calista lives," Ariel said.

"I'll ask the fish," said Flounder, swimming off.

"I'll ask my musicians." Sebastian scuttled away, racing across the ocean floor.

"Atlantica is so large," King Triton said thoughtfully. "There has to be an easier way. Where is my royal herald?"

"Here I am, sire!" A sea horse holding a

conch-shell trumpet suddenly appeared.

"Please call out to all the citizens of Atlantica," the king told him. "Ask for their help in finding a mermaid named Calista!"

"Right away, sire." The herald bowed.

Immediately, the sea horse swam to the center of Atlantica with Ariel and King Triton. He blew loudly on his trumpet.

"Hear ye! Hear ye!" he announced. "Anyone who knows the whereabouts of young Calista the mermaid, please see King Triton. Immediately!"

Two voices suddenly called out. "Ariel! Ariel! You're here!"

Alana and Aquata swarmed around Ariel. Then they turned to King Triton. "We heard your herald," said Alana.

"And we can help!" added Aquata. "We know where Calista lives. It's where the sargassum seaweed grows."

"No, no. You're thinking of Malista, not Calista!" said Alana. "You're confusing two mermaids."

"No, I'm not."

"Yes, you are!"

"Calista! Calista!"

"Malista! Malista!"

Meanwhile, merpeople and sea creatures began crowding all around. Everyone talked at once.

"Marissa? It's Marissa you're looking for?" shouted a teenage merman. "She lives by the Coral Line."

"Oh! You're searching for Coraline?" said

an old sea turtle, slowly. "Her family moved to Pacifica."

Shouts and cries rang out, suggesting different names and places.

Aquata turned to Alana. "How odd," she said. "They sound just like us."

Ariel pushed back her hair in frustration. This was getting them nowhere.

Finally, King Triton raised his trident. "We are looking for CALISTA," he thundered. "Does anyone know where CALISTA lives?"

"Oh, *Calista*," everyone said at once. They all grew quiet.

Suddenly, Sebastian's voice rang out. "I know where she lives!"

The crowd parted as Sebastian raced across the ocean floor, dodging tails and fins.

"I know, too!" Flounder swam over merpeople's heads.

Ariel clapped. "Are you sure?"

"My musicians are positive," said Sebastian.

"My fish friends, too," said Flounder.

"It's the green house!" added Sebastian.

"With the vine swing," Flounder put in.

They spoke at the same time. "That's where Calista lives for sure!"

Chapter Eight

Calista's house was not far from the palace.

"I'm surprised she didn't hear everyone arguing," King Triton said as he and Ariel floated up to a simple vine cottage.

"King Triton!" a merwoman exclaimed behind them. She swam up to where they were. "You're here to see me?" Her eyes were wide with wonder.

"Excuse us for intruding," Ariel said. "We are looking for a young mermaid named Calista."

The woman gasped. "Calista is my daughter!"

"Is she here?" Ariel asked. "We'd like to talk to her."

The woman bowed slightly. "I just arrived home myself, but, of course, she should be inside. Please come with me."

They all swam into the cottage. "Calista!" her mother called. "Are you here?"

"Mother!" Calista floated out through her bedroom door. You're home! I have to tell you something—"

She stopped short when she saw Ariel and King Triton.

"It's the king!" she whispered. Her eyes fell to the seafloor.

"Calista." Her mother swam over to her. "King Triton and Princess Ariel need to talk to you."

"Hello, Calista," Ariel said gently. "It's nice to meet you."

"H-h-hello," Calista stammered.

"We're looking for a human girl named Laurel," Ariel told her. "Do you know her?"

"L-L-Laurel?" Calista stammered again.

"Don't worry, you're not in trouble," King Triton said. "We just want to know where Laurel is."

Calista looked down nervously.

"Laurel's father is very worried," Ariel added.

Finally, Calista nodded. "I don't want anyone to worry," she said softly.

Calista waved for everyone to follow her. They swam to a small bedroom. It was cozy and very pretty, with shells and sea gems scattered around a clamshell bed.

"It's all right," Calista called. "You can come out now."

A noise came from under the bed. Ariel bent down.

Slowly, Laurel crawled out. First her head. Then her shoulders. And then her tail!

Ariel gasped. "Laurel!" she exclaimed. "You're a mermaid!"

The girl stared at Ariel in surprise. "So are you!"

Ariel sat next to Laurel on the bed. "It's a

long story. But I am King Triton's daughter."
Ariel pointed to Laurel's tail. "How did this
happen?"

"It's so hard to explain," said Laurel. "But
it all started this morning. I came to visit
Calista on the beach. Of course I was
wearing my shell necklace. I hadn't taken
it off since Calista gave it to me. I waded
into the water and watched Calista diving
around the waves. She was having so much
fun. I wished I could do that, too. I wished
I could be a mermaid. And all of a sudden,
my necklace lit up. Then both of my legs
disappeared, and I had a mermaid's tail! I
was so excited!"

"Me, too!" Calista grinned. "We knew that
the star shell must be magical. We thought

all we'd have to do was wish again, and Laurel would turn human."

"So we dived down to Atlantica," Laurel continued. "And Calista showed me everything. First, we went to the Blue Whale Playground and slid down the octopus slide twice. Then we explored a cavern where eels lit up like shooting stars."

Calista nodded. "Laurel told me she had

to get back for a singing lesson. But before she left, I wanted to show her the sea-grass garden."

"It was beautiful!" said Laurel. "It was like being in a meadow, but underwater! Then I swam into a . . . a . . . what is it called, Calista?"

"A slipstream," Calista said. "Laurel was stuck in it. I grabbed her arm."

"But my necklace got caught on a sea branch," Laurel continued. "The slipstream carried it away!" Laurel blinked back tears. "We didn't know what to do. Without it, I couldn't change back into a human."

"So we were waiting for my mother," Calista said. "We were going to tell her the whole story."

"We didn't mean to worry anyone." Laurel sniffled.

"We were just so scared!" the girls said together.

Suddenly, Calista's eyes opened wide. "Oh!" she exclaimed, staring at Ariel. She swam closer. "Princess Ariel! You have it. You have the star shell. Now Laurel can go home!"

"Wait a minute," Ariel said. "I don't think—"

But Calista was already placing her hand on the necklace. "I wish for Laurel to be human again!"

Chapter Nine

Nothing happened.

"What?" asked Calista, confused. "Why didn't it work?"

"Maybe I need to go to the surface," Laurel suggested. "And then the wish will come true."

"Wait!" Ariel called.

But Calista had already grabbed Laurel's hand. They floated out the window, and up, up, up.

The friends popped their heads out of the water at the surface. A second later, Ariel joined them.

"Still nothing!" said Laurel. "Maybe if we swim closer to shore . . ."

"Stop!" Ariel held up her hand. "I was trying to tell you about the legend of the star shell."

Quickly, she explained the story and the childhood rhyme. "You can only make one wish on a star shell. You already did that when Laurel wanted to be a mermaid. The magic is gone."

Laurel looked stunned. "You mean I'll never be a human again?"

Ariel turned to King Triton, who had also surfaced. "Can you change her back, Father?"

The king shook his head. "Even my trident can't undo a wish made on a star shell. But there is one more piece to the legend."

"There is?" Laurel asked eagerly.

King Triton smiled as Ariel handed him the star shell. "You don't remember the end to the rhyme, do you?"

"I knew there was more to it!" Ariel exclaimed.

King Triton recited:

"One star, one shell, one wish is all.
To undo a wish the shell must fall."

He looked at both girls. "You must break the shell. And the wish will be reversed."

Laurel and Calista exchanged glances. "Then there'll be no more star shell," Laurel said slowly.

"You won't ever be a mermaid again," Calista added. "Not even a chance of more magic." She sniffed, then squeezed Laurel's hand. "Oh, please don't go! We'll have so much fun under the ocean! We'll do every-thing together."

She turned to her mother, who had also

come to the surface. "And she could stay with us? Couldn't she, Mother?"

"Laurel doesn't belong here," her mother said gently. "She needs to be with her father."

Laurel nodded. "I have to be human again." She hugged Calista. "But I will miss you!"

Ariel swam over and put an arm around each girl. "You two can still see each other. You can play by the ocean, Laurel. And Calista can meet you on a rock, just like I do with my sisters."

"That's true!" Laurel gave a little splash in the water. "And I can bring you more treats from the bakery."

"And I can give you more shells!" said Calista. "Even if they aren't magic."

Ariel glanced up at the sun. "It's almost time for the concert," she reminded Laurel.

Together, everyone swam closer to the shore. They stopped by the large flat rock. Laurel's father, who was still waiting where Ariel and King Triton had left him, stood up anxiously. He squinted, but he was too far away to see what was happening.

"You should go first," King Triton told Ariel. He raised his trident high in the air.

In a flash, Ariel was human.

She climbed onto the rock. Then she helped Calista and Laurel up, too. "Here," she said to Laurel, handing her the star shell. "It's up to you now."

Laurel lifted the star shell up. Sun rays shone through it, and it glowed brighter.

Then she brought it down against the rock's hard surface. It shattered. Bits of shell scattered everywhere. Laurel reached to brush some pieces off her mermaid tail. But instead, she was dusting off her legs.

"I'm human!" she cried. Laurel hugged Calista tight. "It was a wonderful adventure," she whispered. "And we'll see each other all the time. I promise."

Ariel helped Laurel to shore. Immediately, Mr. Hansen rushed over to hug his daughter. "Laurel! Thank goodness you're safe. I was so worried."

Laurel buried her face in his chest. "Oh, Daddy. I missed you! And I have so much to tell you."

She turned to look back out at the sea.

Calista was still there, with her mother and King Triton. The young mermaid waved to Laurel from the waves. Then they all dove back under the water.

"It was the best adventure ever," Laurel whispered.

Chapter Ten

The sun was setting over the ocean. Streaks of red and gold lit up the sky.

"It's beautiful, isn't it, Eric?" Ariel said.

"Lovely," Eric agreed. He put an arm around Ariel and held her close.

"Come on, come on!" Sebastian scuttled between them. "Enough romance! There's a concert about to start."

It was true. All around the beach people scurried about.

"Excuse us!" students called, carrying a banner stretched across two poles. It read:

Village School Royal Concert! All Are Welcome!

They planted the sign firmly in the sand.

Ariel could see her sisters floating on the waves not far away. Alana and Aquata lifted Calista on their shoulders. Ariel smiled. Everything was working out perfectly!

Miss Summers had planned for the

concert to be at the school. But Ariel had asked the teacher if they could move it to the beach. And Miss Summers had agreed! So now, Laurel could share her music with Calista.

Laurel stopped by Ariel on her way to the stage. "I can see Calista," she whispered. "She's watching us right now!"

A moment later, Miss Summers stood in front of the audience. "Welcome, everyone, to our royal concert. I'd like to introduce our first solo performer—Laurel!"

Smiling, Laurel stepped into place. Ariel and Eric were sitting next to Laurel's father. He beamed proudly.

"Thank you so much, Princess," he said, "for finding my daughter."

Then Laurel began to sing. "Oh, the waves may roll. The fish may swim. The gentle surf may meet the shore . . ."

"Hey, it's my favorite song!" Eric said. "The Song of the Sea!"

When it was over, the audience rose to their feet. Everyone clapped. "That was perfect!" Ariel cheered.

The concert continued well into the evening. Teachers lit lanterns, and stars twinkled in the dark sky. Finally, after the last song had been performed and the applause had faded, Ariel, Laurel, and Mr. Hansen slipped away from the crowd and over to the water.

"I have a present for you and Calista," Ariel told Laurel. She handed Laurel a

brand-new necklace made from star-shell pieces. Earlier, she'd gone back to the ocean rock and picked up the pieces of broken shell. Now they were strung into two glittering necklaces.

Laurel gasped. "It's beautiful!"

Calista swam to shore. "Your song was amazing," she told Laurel. Then Ariel gave

the young mermaid her matching necklace. "I love it!" Calista breathed. "Thank you, Princess Ariel."

Together, Laurel and Calista slipped on the necklaces. They twinkled in the starlight.

Mr. Hansen and Ariel watched happily as both girls started giggling and splashing in the water. A moment later, Prince Eric walked over and placed his arm around Ariel's shoulders.

What if, right now, a shooting star fell? Ariel wondered. And turned a regular seashell into a magical one? What would she wish for?

She'd wish for this moment to last.

Don't miss the next Disney Princess Jewel Story!

Cinderella
The Lost Tiara

When a royal messenger brings word that Cinderella's new grandmother-in-law is coming to visit, everyone in the castle scrambles to prepare. Cinderella wants everything to be perfect for her first royal guest! As a special surprise, she decides to wear the beautiful tiara Grandmama sent as a gift. But when Cinderella goes to the royal vault, she discovers that the crown is missing! Can she find it before Grandmama notices it is gone?